Lindsay Barrett George

The Secret

Greenwillow Books

An Imprint of HarperCollins*Publishers*

"Can you keep a secret?"
said Mr. Snail to the mouse.

"Yes, I can," said the mouse.
"Then listen . . . ," said Mr. Snail.

But . . .

the mouse

squeaked the secret to the beetle.

The beetle

pinched it to the turtle.

The turtle grumbled it to the fish.

who swished it to the frog.

The frog

croaked it to the salamander

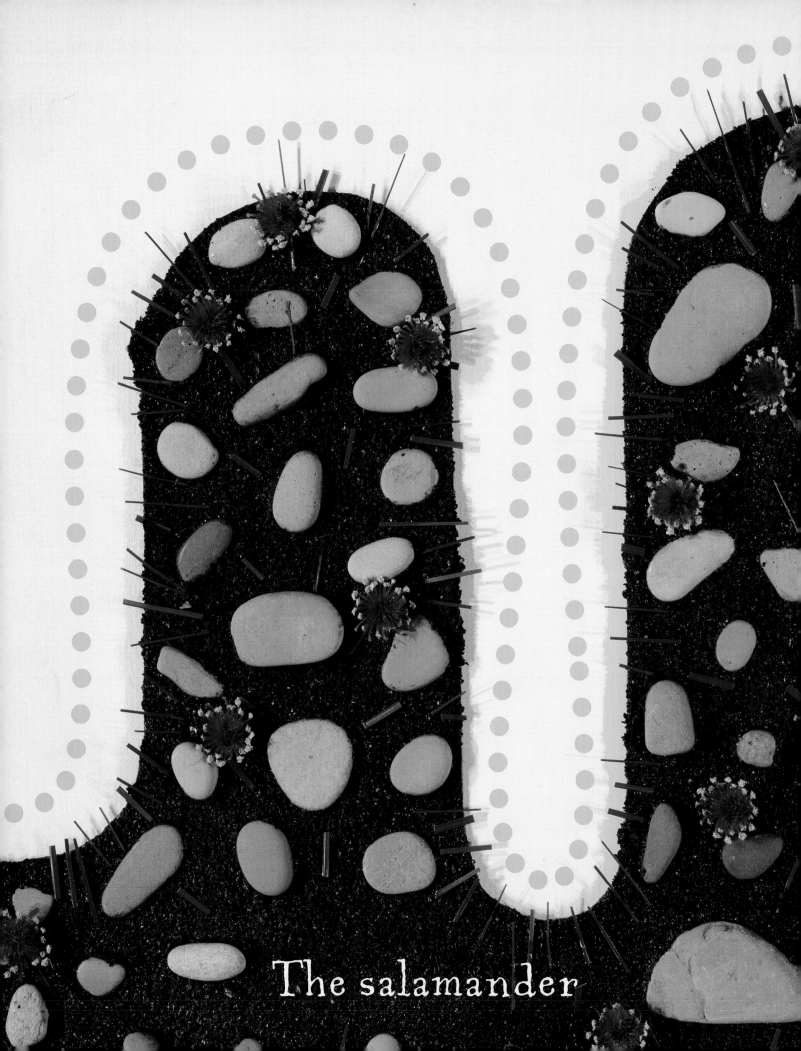

The salamander

wiggled it to the moth.

The moth shook it to the bee.

who buzzed it to the caterpillar.

The caterpillar

tickled it to the worm.

The worm

hummed it to the chickadee.

The chickadee sang it to the cricket,

who chirped it to the snake.

The snake

hissed it to the chipmunk.

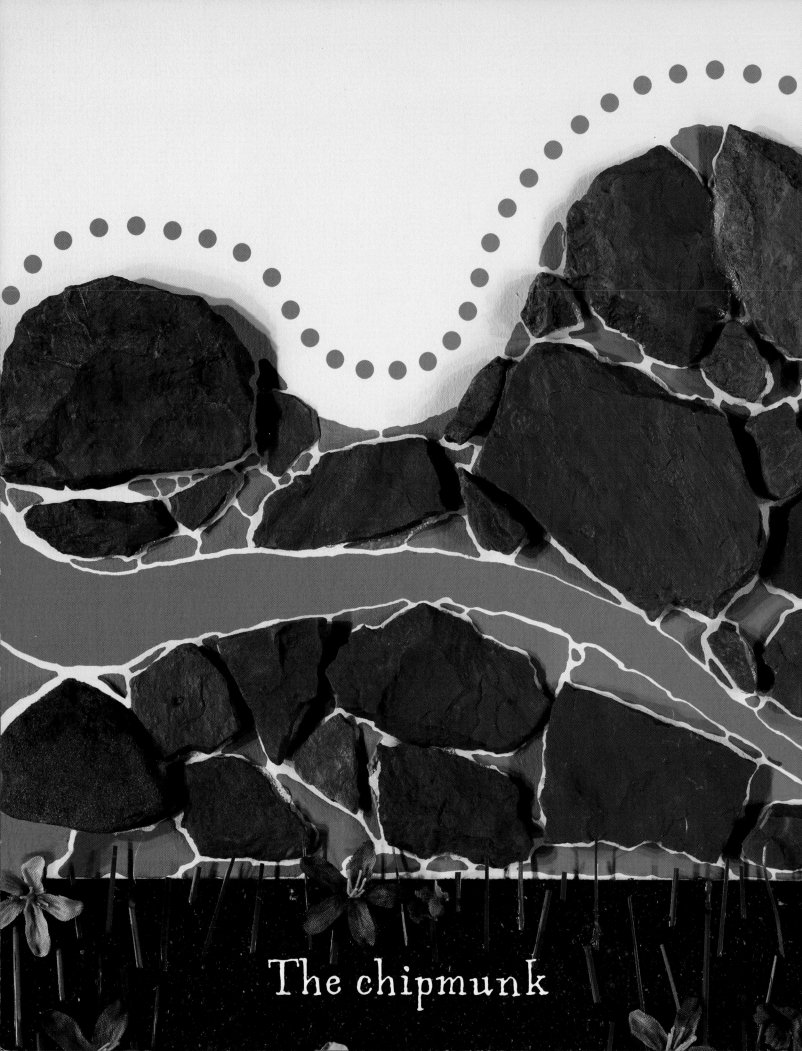

The chipmunk

chattered it to the spider,

and the spider
clicked the secret
to Miss Snail,

who turned around
and whispered,

To Sylvie, with appreciation

The Secret. Copyright © 2005 by Lindsay Barrett George. All rights reserved. Manufactured in China by South China Printing Company Ltd. www.harperchildrens.com. The art was prepared digitally using collages of natural materials and watercolors. The text type is Aunt Mildred.

Library of Congress Cataloging-in-Publication Data. George, Lindsay Barrett. The secret / by Lindsay Barrett George. p. cm. "Greenwillow Books." Summary: Mr. Snail tells a mouse his secret, and the mouse passes it on to the beetle who tells the turtle, and so on, until the secret gets back to Miss Snail. ISBN 0-06-029598-8 (trade). ISBN 0-06-029600-3 (lib. bdg.) [1. Snails—Fiction. 2. Animals—Fiction. 3. Secrets—Fiction.] I. Title. PZ7.G29334Se 2005 [E]—dc22 2003056862